DEXTER
Fittin' In

Stepping through life,
one paw at a time

Dedicated to: CPL David Webb Jr, our *"Devil Dog"*
whose light continues to burn brightly… *Semper Fi.*

MICHELE WEBB

PAGE PUBLISHING, INC.
Conneaut Lake, PA

First originally published by Page Publishing 2020

ISBN 978-1-6624-0247-0 (pbk)
ISBN 978-1-6624-0248-7 (digital)

Printed in the United States of America

Chapter 1

Hey, I Just Got Picked!

Hi. I'm not sure where I am, or even who I am. I am in a really big room with lots and lots of dogs. By the way, I am a dog—well, really, a puppy. There are all kinds of dogs—big ones, small ones, hairy ones, skinny ones, some in cages, and then there is like a bowl in the middle of the room, and that's where I am. Lots of big two leggers have been in and out all day. They come in and look at the dogs in the kennels (they look like cages to me), and then they look at us.

I don't really know what is going on, but sometimes they take us out of the cages or bowl, and the two leggers hold us and make funny noises. Sometimes I get scared. So today this pretty lady walks in, and she has a dog with her. He doesn't look happy to be here, but he has a cool mustache. The lady looks in a few cages and then goes into a room. I see the people taking dogs from the kennel in to her, and then they come back. The lady comes out, and she looks kind of sad. Another two legger walks up to her and points at us in the big, big bowl in the middle of the room. The lady looks down, and she smiles at me. I do my best to smile back. She bends down and picks me up.

Next thing I know, we go into the room, and she looks at the dog that came with her and says, "Reilly, what do you think?"

Well, this dog, Reilly, looks over at me, walks over, and sniffs my face, and then he turns his head and looks out the door. He looks bored. Oh no, I don't think he likes me. I start to get sad.

The next thing I know, the lady laughs and says, "Well, at least you looked at him, and I think he's the one."

The lady looks over at the other two legger and says the best words in the world, "We'll take him."

Okay, so I don't know exactly what that means, but I am pretty sure it is a good thing, 'cause the lady picks me up, grabs a rope, and they pay for me (not sure what that is all about), and we leave the big room and go outside and get into this big boxy thing with seats.

At this point, I am shaking like a leaf. It is cold outside, and I am scared. I am pretty sure she's a nice person, but I really don't know what is happening or where I am going. The lady puts Reilly and me on the seat next to her. She pushes some buttons, turns a few knobs, and we start to get warm, and then we start to move. The box on wheels is moving.

I look at Reilly and ask him, "What is this thing?"

He rolls his eyes and snorts, "It's a car."

Isn't he smart? So we are moving a lot, and I guess my tummy isn't ready for this 'cause next thing I know, I make a mess on the floor. But the lady just pets me and says, "It's okay, you will be all right."

It seems like we ride forever, but probably not too long. We stop, we go, we turn, we go slowly, we go fast, we are on smooth roads, and then we are on a rock road. Next thing, she pulls up to a building (I didn't know this was our house) and pushes another button.

She drives into this building and stops the car. Reilly jumps out and goes in front of the car, and the lady picks me up and walks up front, and we all go through the door and into a pretty room.

The lady says, "Hey, we're home."

And then sets me down on the floor. Well, the next thing I know, a giant comes around the corner and says, "That's the new puppy? What's he known for and how much did he cost?"

The lady laughs and says, "Don't worry, he didn't break the bank, and he is a beagle/dachshund mix."

Then the giant stoops down and picks me up and says, "He's a good-looking dog and has a solid build."

I don't know what that means, but he likes me. I think I like him too.

Today has been a good day. I think I am going to like my new home.

Chapter 2

My New Litter (Family)—and a New Name!

Hey, it's me again. I am excited, happy, and jittery all at the same time! The lady is now my new mom, and the big giant (he's alpha around here) is my new dad. And guess what is even better than that? I got a new big brother, and he is pretty cool looking. And get this, his name is not just Reilly, it is Corporal Reilly Webb. Slick, huh? He keeps looking at me kind of funny, and when I go sit by him, he gets up and moves, but you know what? I think we are gonna be best, best friends.

So my mom says, "I am going to take you to your room. Once you get trained [not sure what that means], you will be able to walk all around the house."

And let me tell you about this house—it is HUGE! There are rooms where there is food; there is a room with a big screen that talks all the time (actually, these screens are all through the house). There are rooms with big, tall beds that I can't reach (but Reilly can); there are a couple of rooms with funny-looking bowls that water swishes all around in. But Mom takes me to a room with two big machines that hum. She puts clothes (I don't use these) in them. I don't know why, but there must be a good reason.

Then Mom puts me into a cage (she calls it a crate), but I can't get out. There is a warm blanket and some toys in here. I have to stay until she comes with Reilly to take me outside. I really don't like it when they leave me, kinda scary, so I better get trained fast. It's so funny; we go outside, and I have to go potty right away, and you know what? Mom gets all happy, claps her hands, and jumps up and down. I guess that is good. Reilly just looks at me and goes way off into the yard, sniffs around, and then raises his leg and goes potty. Way too cool!

We go back inside, and for a little while, I get to sit in the real big room with a fire stove that keeps us warm.

Dad asks Mom, "Hey, what are you gonna call him?"

Mom looks at me and says, "I think his name will be Dexter Eli Webb."

Dad says, "Where did 'that' come from?"

Mom says, "Well, he looks like a Dexter, and we got him December 31, which is close to my mom's birthday, but we can't call him Elizabeth, so he will be Eli."

Dad nods and puts on his spectacles and begins reading his paper.

Mom looks at me and says, "Welcome to the family, Dexter Eli Webb."

Yeah, me, I gotta a family and a cool older brother to boot! I'm beginning to feel the love.

Chapter 3

Learning the Ropes

Hey, everybody. It's me, Dexter. I love my name. I really love it when my mom says it. So I've been doing good. I don't have to spend as much time in the cage 'cause I've been going to potty or, as Mom says, tinkle and bobo's outside. I do my very best to hold my stomach so I don't make messes. Mom is good about it, but Dad just looks at me and makes a face. Not sure what it means, but I'm trying my best.

So Reilly tells me we have things we do every day and I need to be ready. So of course, first we have to go potty. This happens a lot of times during day, just so you know. Next, we get to eat. I am so happy. I used to share my dish with a lot of others, but no more, I got my own. So Mom fixes us food and water and then leaves us to eat. So guess who eats real fast? You got it, Reilly. And you know what, when he's done, he helps himself to my food. Aha, guess who's also learning to eat fast.

Next, we go outside again in a big space that we can run in and have fun. I just follow Reilly 'cause he's cool and my big brother. So one minute he's right in front of me, and the next, *wham!*—he's flying across the space chasing a squirrel. I mean he is flying. The squirrel runs up a tree at the last second, and Reilly is mad barking at him. Wow! I've never seen this, way cool.

Next thing, Reilly comes over to me panting hard with his tongue sticking out and says, "Never let a squirrel or rabbit run free in our yard. It is our job to chase them down. Got it?"

I'm like, "Yep, sure, okay, but, Reilly, can you show me how?"

So guess who watches Reilly every time we go outside. First, survey the landscape. Next, identify the target (which means squirrel or rabbit). Reilly is a Yorkie, and they get very specific and a bit bossy (but don't tell him I said it), then you get real still, and once they move, you take off like a rocket into space and try and snag their legs. It's kind of funny 'cause Reilly always misses them by just a little and the squirrels then go halfway up the tree and turn around, and it looks like they wave at him. I laugh (very quietly), but now I know how to chase them.

It's kinda fun and good exercise. Reilly says we need to stay strong and in shape, so we do. I love my brother, and I think he likes me too. The next big thing to learn is to sound the alarm. Yep, I didn't know what that meant either, and I told Reilly, and he just rolled his eyes and shook his head. So he explained that when we hear this music in the house, we have to run our very hardest to the door and *bark, bark, bark*; even after Mom or Dad get there, Reilly says we should keep barking. Reilly's barks sounds cool, but mine is like *jip, jip, jip*. But you know what, I do my very best *jip*! Mom and Dad tell us to be quiet, and Reilly doesn't look happy but stops, so I do too. I hide behind Mom or Dad 'cause I'm scared of strangers. Not Reilly, he is right beside them. Wow, I can't wait till I have his confidence. I'm not there yet, but I'm learning lots every day.

Chapter 4

My Mentor, Reilly–I Want to Be Him When I Grow Up

So it's me again, and I gotta let you know I am loving my family. Yeah, sometimes I make mistakes or get in trouble, but they love me! Even Reilly, though he acts like he doesn't. He tells me the reason they adopted me is 'cause Mom has to travel a lot and he is left alone a lot. So Mom has read that it will be a good idea for them to get a puppy (ME!) to keep him company. I agree, but not Reilly. He calls me a pain in the "you know what." But I think Mom is right; Reilly needs me, and I am so slap happy to be here it's crazy. And let me tell you something, Reilly knows a lot about everything. He says I need to learn the ropes and there a few key sounds/noises you need to know. One I mentioned before is the doorbell or music in the house. Anytime—and I mean *anytime*—it rings, we have to run full speed, barking the entire way to the door.

See, this is important for Mom and Dad to know strangers are on the property. Could be good, could be bad, we don't know, but our job is to sound the alarm. Next are the kitchen sounds, either the refrigerator door opening or the oven. Man, run like you are being chased by a crazy cat; food is usually dropped on the floor and tossed to you. Be ready, prepared, and in place. Hey, this is stuff you gotta know! Most important when we are home alone and the door is opening, repeat number one and run, bark, jump up and down, and get excited, 'cause either Mom or Dad or both are getting home and we need to greet them with barks or joy and tails a-wagging.

Mom always says, "Hey, boys, how ya doing?"

I love her. There are other sounds that are not so good, like Thunder. I don't even know what it is, but man, it's a big, loud noise that shakes the house. I run under the bed and put my paws over my head. It scares me, but NOT Reilly.

He sits in the window and stares outside. He's crazy. I whine and beg him to get under the bed with me. He just gives me the Reilly look and stays where he is. I love Reilly, but sometimes, I think he is crazy. But really, he is my hero; nothing scares him. And when the thunder goes away and I come out, he grins at me and says, "Come on."

Reilly says the only way for me to stop being scared is to face my fears! I don't know about that and don't plan to try anytime soon, but I tell him okay. I don't want him to think I'm a wimp, but I kinda am. Man, am I lucky. I have the bestest teacher in the world. I am learning lots, and it's okay to be afraid and follow the leader in your pack (unless they are cray-cray). And guess what, they may be tough on you or push you to be better and try harder, and that's okay. Reilly acts real tough, but I know from my heart to my paws, he is beginning to like me. I know I love him. When I grow up, I want to be just like Reilly.

Chapter 5

Wow, I Got Lots of Family and Friends

Hey there, it's me, Dexter, again. Life is so good and way better than I thought. Sometimes fittin' in is kinda tricky, but I just love my brother, Reilly, and my two-legged parents. They are so nice to me, especially Mom. She lets me sit by her and rubs my belly. She also goes into this box and gives us treats. I don't even have to do a trick; well, we do have to sit, but that's pretty easy. So one day we are in the big room with that talking box, and Reilly hears a noise and starts barking like crazy, so of course, I join him, and in walks an even bigger two legger. He's taller than Dad is. I am scared. I run behind Mom.

She smiles and says, "What's up, Poot?"

That big giant does not look or sound like a Poot, and Reilly is giving him the stink eye.

Well, guess what? You've guessed it. He walks over and bends down over me and says, "Where'd you get him, and what's his name?"

Mom tells him that she got me a bit ago and my name is Dexter.

The big, goofy giant grins and says, "Detter."

Hello, did you not hear Mom? She said Dexter.

Then get this, he picks me up. Help, I am in the sky. Help. He just laughs and gives me a little hug and puts me down. I run behind Mom 'cause I'm scared, but I kinda like him.

He then looks over and says, "Hey, Rye."

Rye, who the heck is Rye? But he reaches down and pats Reilly's head. Reilly continues to give him the stink eye. Huh, must be a story there, but I'm not pushing that tonight.

I ask Reilly, "Hey, who's that, and what's his name?"

And Reilly snorts and says, "Big Darney, and he is Mom's son. She has another one, but he is in heaven."

I don't know what that means, but Reilly says it's important and he is named after him. Wow, that is pretty cool—both our names come from Mom's family.

Well, Big Darney talks to Mom awhile, and then he goes into the food room and starts getting stuff out and guess what? There goes Reilly, into the food room with Big Darney.

I jump up and chase Reilly and say, "Hey, what's up? You told me you don't like him."

Reilly gives me a side look and says, "I don't like him, but whenever he eats, he always drops food or tosses some to me, so I might not like him, but I'm not stupid. Ha ha."

Reilly is too much. I love learning from him.

So we go outside with Mom so she can sit on the porch and we can roam the yard and go potty, chase bugs and squirrels, or just lie down in the grass. Next thing I know, Reilly takes off at lightning speed across the yard. I start running too.

"Hey, Reilly, slow down. Where you goin'?" And I see this tall lady with white hair and a white dog that looks like he could be Reilly's cousin.

He comes running over to me, and Reilly intercepts and knocks him away from me.

The white dog says, "Dang, Reilly, what's up? And who is he?"

Reilly says, "Look, Murphy, this is my new brother, and you better not bother him."

"Gee," Murphy says, "I was just gonna say hi and sniff him."

Reilly nods and says, "Okay, but member what I told you."

And then Reilly goes over to the lady, and she picks him up and says, "How's my buddy?"

Reilly smiles and looks happy. Wow, this is weird. Then Murphy starts toward me, but guess what, I take off at the speed of light and run to Mom!

She smiles and picks me up and says, "These are our neighbors, Dexter."

Mom walks over to the lady and shows me to her, and they talk. I just sit and be quiet, 'cause I don't want to get down and deal with Murphy. I don't think he is my friend yet.

Soon Mom and the lady stop talking, and she puts me down, and the lady puts Reilly down and Mom says, "Come on, boys, let's go home."

Reilly and I take off running toward our house. I look back and see Murphy doing the same, and then he looks back at me and barks. I guess maybe one day, when I get bigger, we can be friends.

Chapter 6

You Gotta Learn Some Stuff on Your Own, but I'm Fittin' In

Hey there, everybody. It's me, Dexter. I'm still here and learning lots every day. We have had some experiences this week. Mom takes me and Reilly downstairs so she can wash clothes. Guess not for us 'cause we don't wear them.

Anyway, she says, "Dexter, its' time for you to go up and down the stairs on your own."

I don't know exactly what stairs are, but I guess I'm gonna find out. So we head to the hallway, and instead of picking me up, Mom puts me at the top of this cliff! Seriously, there I am at the top of this cliff, and it has a whole bunch of steps that I guess I gotta go down. Of course, here comes Reilly. He looks at me and then just bounds down the steps.

About halfway down, he turns and looks at me! Well, I ain't crazy. I start backing up, and guess what?

Mom pushes me toward the cliff again and says, "Come on, Dexter, you can do this!"

Ah, heck, no, I can't. I think she's crazy! I look at her for help, and she says, "Let's go," and pushes my bottom! Yikes, here I go. I know this is it. I'm gonna fall and not get up. I'm gonna roll over and over and over.

"Oh, stop, Dexter. You're are being a baby," says you know who (Reilly). Then he says, "Put both front paws on the stairs and let your weight carry you. If you stop whining, you can do this."

Yep, this comes from Mr. Know-It-All.

I look back, and Mom is looking at me, so I guess, I can only try.

So I push my paws real hard and land on the first step, and then, my bottom is there. I try again, and I get to the next one and then the next and then the next, then oops, I kinda tumble and roll, and hey, I'm at the bottom. I did it.

Mom is so happy. She says, "Good job, Dexter. You did it! See, sometimes you have to just try really hard to work on something you're scared of, but you can conquer it! Good job."

Well, I am a bit dizzy, but kinda proud. I did it. I am so excited.

I say, "Hey, Reilly, I made it down the stairs! I'm getting better every day, so what do you think about that!"

Reilly just gets a funny look on his face and says, "Yep, Dex, you did good, but guess what?"

"What, Reilly, what?"

Reilly says, "Now you gotta go up the stairs!"

"Huh? Are you kidding me? No way, that is not true." He's just being mean, right?

"Hey, Mom, Reilly's being mean. I don't have to go up the steps, do I?"

Mom looks down, rubs my head, and says, "Reilly is right. We have to go back upstairs. We only come down here to wash clothes!"

"Oh boy, I gotta rest for a minute. I don't know that I can do this."

Mom says, "Sure you can, Dexter. You can do anything you put your mind to. Reilly had to learn!"

"Yeah, but, Mom, Reilly knows everything. I don't think I can do it!"

Mom says, "Just try, one paw at a time."

So you know who goes ahead of me and trots up the stairs, looks back, and says, "Two paws at a time and go fast."

"Okay, Reilly, I can do this." Here I go, one step, two, three four (hey, I'm moving), gulp, oops, I missed the stair and hit my chest. Oh no, I'm' gonna fall all the way down.

"Keep going, Dexter. You're almost there," says Reilly.

"Okay, let me get my paws together." Here I go, step five, six, seven, eight… Hey, I'm at the top…I'm not letting go. I am scared I'm gonna fall. I look back, and guess what? Mom is right there and is standing behind me the whole way. I didn't know she was there and had my back. I am now scooting across the floor and letting my heart slow down. Wow, that was so scary, but I did it! I am learning stuff every day! I'm feeling tired, scared, and crazy, but kinda proud.

Sometimes we have to challenge ourselves to do stuff that looks hard, but if we keep trying, we can win! Fittin' in ain't easy, but it's important to do your best. I think that my family is so cool! They expect things of me but give me examples and have my back. I feel blessed, just like Mom says every day.

Chapter 7

Adventure 1: Field Trip to the Vet

Hey, hey, it's me, Dexter! I've been doing real good. I know how to go potty (yep, even lift my leg), bark when the doorbell rings, chase squirrels, climb stairs, and do all kinds of cool stuff. I'm feeling pretty good about myself. I've even tried to poke my chest out like Reilly does. It didn't quite look right, but hey, I tried.

Anyway, all is going good, and then Mom says we gotta go on a few adventures this month.

I look at Reilly and say, "Adventure, what is that?"

He just says, "Relax, no big deal."

"Well, okay then." No big deal, right?

So we get up early the next day, and Mom says we are going to the vet.

I look around and say, "Huh? Reilly, what's a vet?"

He says, "It's the dog doctor, dodo!"

I ask, "Is it fun? What do we get to do there? Come on, Reilly, tell me something."

He just says, "Wait and see."

Sometimes I wanna punch him (giggle, but I'm not crazy). So Mom puts on our leashes (so we don't run off) and puts us in the car. Well, I hope you member that I don't do good in cars! I get real scared, start shaking, and I guess I whine a little (okay, maybe a lot), and my tummy hurts, actually feels like it's doing somersaults. Help, help, I whine.

Mom reaches over and says, "Relax, we'll be there before you know it!"

"Yeah, right!"

Well, after what seemed like forever, we stop and get out of the car. Thank you, Jesus. We are on solid ground. Mom takes us into a big building, and holy moly, what is going on? There are two weird-looking dogs and a cat. A big cat that is staring at me! Mom goes to the desk and starts talking to a lady. Reilly just looks around, and I hide between Mom's feet.

Next, she walks us across the room and sits down. Guess who is still staring at me? The big cat! I think it wants to get me! I don't like this cat at all.

So now here comes this lady with paper in her hand and shouts out, "Dexter and Reilly."

Mom says, "Here we are."

And the lady says, "Let's weigh them!"

Not sure what that means, but when Mom weighs herself at home, she gets mad and calls it the devil. Oh well, here we go. Mom picks me up and sits me on the scale.

The lady says, "Eight pounds."

Then I get off, and they weigh Reilly. I'm thinking what's the big deal; that wasn't hard, and it didn't even hurt.

Next we go into a room, and an old man comes in and says, "Now what do we have here?"

I wanna say a dog, well a puppy, but you know what I mean.

Mom says, "This is Dexter, our new puppy, and he needs to get checked and shots."

Shots? What are shots? Nobody is telling me, so then this guy starts looking at my teeth, checks my back, and rubs my legs, and then he sticks this tube in my hiney. Hey, buddy, not cool, watch it!

He just smiles and pulls the tube out and says his temperature is good. Next he gets these tools out of a drawer adds some stuff in them and tells Mom to hold me.

I'm thinking, *This ain't bad. He's just going to*—YIKES, Help, I just got stabbed in the neck by this crazy man Really? Mom, help!

Mom just rubs my neck and says, "The shots give you medicine to help you."

Well, I don't know about this. I don't think anything that helps should hurt so much! I don't like this place. So then they put Reilly on the table and get ready to do the same.

I yell, "Run, Reilly, the man is crazy."

But guess who sits perfectly still and doesn't even flinch when getting stabbed. Really, Reilly, Really?

Mom walks us out and gives the lady some paper, and we get in the car and go home.

I am so upset about the shots that I forget to be nervous in the car. We get home. Mom takes off my leash, and I run as fast as I can under the bed. I know she says this is good for me, but I don't like it. I don't like the vet and the big cat that kept staring at me. I tell Reilly I'm never going back there.

And he looks at me and says, "Yeah, you will, 'cause sometimes things that hurt for a minute help us for a long time."

I think about that, and then I get ready to sleep! I do know that Mom loves me and won't do anything to hurt me, I guess even shots. Good night.

Chapter 8

Adventure 2: Going to the Beauties–Can't Be Stinking!

Hey, there, its' me, Dexter here and ready for another new adventure, except the vet. I don't like that place, but other stuff is okay with me. So I guess you know by now I'm learning all kinds of stuff, and one thing I haven't really talked about is being clean. So since I was born, I've been cleaning me. Right? That's why dogs have tongues, and once in a while, we play in the rain or jump in a puddle. Yeah, 'bout that, last time I jumped in the puddle, it felt so good. I was happy. Well, next thing I know, Mom grabbed me and said, "Really, Dexter, you are filthy."

How am I filthy? I feel all wet and gooey. Well, guess she didn't see it that way. Next thing I know, she takes me into the bathroom (see, I know what this is 'cause Reilly taught me how to get drinks out the big bowl, but Mom doesn't know that).

Anyway, she runs with me into the bathroom and puts me in the big bowl on the ground. I know Mom and Dad jump in here and get wet, but hey, whatever. If it makes them feel good, I'm good, but she puts me in. Next, she turns a knob, and water pours out.

"Hey, what are you doing, Mom? I'm getting wet and scared."

She says, "Hush, Dexter, you need a bath."

"Well, yeah, but I was doing that."

Apparently, she isn't listening 'cause she wets my fur and puts smelly stuff on me making bubbles, mom what are you doing? She's not listening and keeps bubbling me up and then pouring water on me. Next she takes me out and stuffs me in a big towel. Well, this doesn't feel too bad, I kind of like it. I smile at mom and am ready to thank her and she says, tomorrow you're going to the beauties. The beauties, what is that? I guess I'll find out.

So we get up early (why do we have to always get up early?), and Mom puts our leashes on and puts us in the car.

I look at Reilly and ask, "Where we going? And I'm scared."

He just looks at me and says, "I think you're gonna like this place."

Okay, if Reilly says so, I'm game. So we get to this building, and Mom takes us inside. First thing I notice is a bunch of cages with all kinds of dogs. I'm getting nervous. Mom starts talking to these ladies, and then they come and get us. Hey, what's going on?

"Mom, where you going?"

Mom smiles and says, "See you guys later."

"What? You're just gonna leave us?"

"Relax," says you know who (Reilly).

So the lady says, "Hey, Reilly, how are you doing, and who is this? You got yourself a little brother."

"Something like that," says Reilly.

So I'm just looking around, and dogs are doing a bunch of strange things in big buckets. Glad it's not me! "Hey, what you are you doing?"

This lady grabs me, drops me in a bucket, and turns on a sprayer. Yikes. AAAAAAAAAAAAAAAAhhhhhhhhhhhhhh, what is happening?

"Reilly, help me." I'm shaking and scared and wet, and I check out Reilly, and he's sitting back, getting wet, with a big old smile. Why isn't he scared?

Well, this torture goes on for a few minutes, and the lady says, "You wanna be clean, don't you, buddy?"

Buddy? I don't know her, and I'm not her buddy. Next thing I know, she puts me in front of a big hot fan. What is she doing? I am not liking this at all. "Lady, let me lone. I just want to go home." So I decide if nobody is gonna help me, I'm gonna just sing out loud—really loud for a long time. I start.

The lady looks and says, "What's wrong?"

But I'm just gonna sing, so what if it sounds like crying.

The lady puts me in a crate and says, "You're done. You can stop now."

Nope, I'm gonna keep singing. I don't care. Next thing I hear is Reilly hissing my name, "Dexter."

I look down, and he's sitting beside a big moose (Saint Bernard) and a funny-looking poodle.

"Dexter, stop whining now."

"Whining? Whining, you think I'm whining? Well, guess what, buddy, I'm singing, and I don't like this place."

"Dexter, shut up. You're embarrassing yourself."

"Embarrass, shamarrass—I don't like this place or you or your friends. I'm scared, and you should be helping me."

"Dexter, you took a bath. Lighten up and stop whining."

So I turn my head and keep singing, which is how Mom finds me when she comes back.

She walks in and says, "Hey, is that my dog making that noise?"

"Yep," says the lady. "He's been carrying on since his bath."

"Oh poor Dexter," says Mom.

"Poor Dexter?" says Reilly. "Really, he has been embarrassing us."

"Come on, guys, let's go. Reilly, you know how to act here 'cause you've been here, but it's new to Dexter, and he has to learn."

If you say so, Mom, but maybe next time, he could go somewhere else. The other dogs laughed, and then I had to shut them up. Ugh, having a little brother is a lot of work."

"You know, Reilly, you may be right, but in the end, you did the right thing. You stuck up and protected your brother. I am proud of you. By the way, you both look and smell great!"

Chapter 9

The Farm-New People and Learnings

So you know I am learning a lot, and every day is a new adventure, and I like most of them. Mom likes to take me and Reilly out to different places, sometimes just to see what is in the world around us.

One day, Mom says, "We're going to the country."

I'm thinking, *We are in the country. We have a really big, big yard with woods in the back. How much more country is there?* But what the heck. If Mom and Reilly are going, I'm good to go too!

So we get in the car, and you know how I feel about that, but the good news is, I don't get sick like when I was a baby. We are only in the car for a little while, and we pull off the street on to a rock road. I stand up and stick my head out the window like Reilly and see miles and miles of plants. They are in really neat rows and are very green and growing.

I say, "Hey, Reilly, what is that?"

Reilly says, "This is a farm, and this is where Daddy is from. They have crops and also some pigs."

"Pigs? Pigs? Real pigs? Will they try to get me? Is Mom crazy? Why are we coming here?"

Reilly just snorts and says, "Chill out."

So we pull up to a house, and Mom takes us out and carries us up to the house. Good thing, 'cause there are a few rough-looking dogs and a cat looking at us. We go inside and meet a nice lady named Granny. Reilly goes over and sits by her, and she smiles and pets him.

She says, "Michele, who is this?"

Mom tells her I'm Dexter.

She smiles and says, "You know you love your dogs."

That makes me smile. I like this lady. Reilly tells me that this is Dad's mom.

"What? No way."

"Yep," says Reilly, it is."

So we stay for a while, and as Mom and Granny talk, I drift to sleep. Next thing I know, Mom lifts us up and says we are heading out now and we go out the back and help me Jesus, there are a bunch of crazy-looking pigs staring at us. Well, I guess I started shaking and crying 'cause Mom holds me and says, "Relax, Dex, it's okay."

Okay? No, it's not. I am scared and want to go home. Next thing I know, Reilly is barking like crazy at a goat. Yep, you heard me, a goat.

Mom says, "Reilly, you better leave that goat alone." Well, you know who doesn't listen and keeps barking.

Granny comes out on the porch and is laughing.

She says, "Michele, you better get that little dog, or that goat is gonna get him."

I look at Mom, and she just kinda shakes her head and walks over by Reilly. So Mr. Big Bark keeps on barking, and the goat starts kicking the dirt and drops it head and is staring at Reilly.

Mom says, "Okay, the fun is over now," and drops me in the car and snatches Reilly up.

She says, "Look here, you crazy Yorkie, when a goat drops its head, it is getting ready to headbutt you and send you flying into space."

OMG, what? "Reilly, are you crazy? Mom just saved you."

Mom puts Reilly in the car and tells Granny we gotta go but will be back soon.

Granny laughs and says, "Come back soon and bring the little fellas with you. They are kinda cute and made me laugh today."

Mom gets into the car and starts driving home.

I look at Reilly and say, "Are you nuts? Weren't you scared?"

Reilly just looks at me and says, "Naw, I would've bitten that goat's ankles. I ain't scared of no goat."

Well, I was kinda proud of my brother 'cause he wasn't scared, but I was afraid 'cause I didn't want him to get hurt.

On the way home, Mom says, "You know, Reilly, barking and teasing that goat wasn't smart, and you could've gotten hurt. Next time, I need you to make better decisions for you and the little one watching you."

Reilly looks at Mom and then me and says, "Okay, I don't want to get hurt and surely don't want Dexter to try that." Then he mumbles something under his breath like; he doesn't move quick enough.

"Hey, Reilly, what'd you say?"

"Nothing, Dexter, nothing. I guess all of us have lessons to learn, even the older ones."

I love my family because I am loved and always learning new things.

Chapter 10

A New Addition to the Family— The Screaming Blanket

You know, I am starting to feel like a true member of my new family. Yeah, there are all kinds of rules—things you have to do and new people and dogs to meet—but all in all, I like my family. Really, I love them. No matter what happens or how many times I make mistakes, I still have a nice place to live, lots of food, and a nice lap to sit on. I don't get as nervous as I used to because Reilly has taught me so many things, and new a lesson has been "paying attention." So I've started doing this more and more, and I notice that Mom, Dad, and big Darney are acting a little strange (you remember him, that is the one they say is Mom's son; I don't know how). And a couple of times, there have been a whole bunch of ladies come to the house with bags and pretty boxes. I'm not sure what they are doing, 'cause me and Reilly get locked in the bedroom. Reilly says it's 'cause some of them are scared of dogs.

"Really, how scary am I?"

Anyway, they seem to stay awhile, eat, laugh, and throw paper around the room. Must be some party or something. But eventually, they go home, and we come back out and try to find the crumbs on the floor (there are quite a few; they are a bit messy).

A few days ago, Mom and Dad brought a big cage into the house and put it into one of the bedrooms and put pretty stuff all inside and on the walls. This is so weird; I don't get it, but something is about to happen. I ask Reilly what's going on, but he says he doesn't know or care. I think he is bluffing, but I really want to know.

So I think, oh well, whatever it is, I'll find out soon enough. Well, before those words came all the way out, Mom comes in the door and tells Dad, "We gotta go. They are admitting her to the hospital. Dad jumps up (that never happens), grabs his coat, and they leave. Reilly and I are just standing there staring after them.

"Hey, Rye, what's going on?"

He sighs and says, "I don't know, Dexter. Go to sleep. We'll figure it out later."

Hmmmm, I still wonder.

The next few days are crazy. Mom and Dad go to work, come home, and then leave until late at night. Weird, right?

One day when they come home, they are happy, dancing, and looking at a picture on the tablet. They seem so happy. What is it that has them so happy? Next thing, Mom gets off work and leaves and doesn't come home until late every night. What the world is it? I know I'm just a dog, but I don't understand.

So today, we are all home sitting in front room watching TV (at least Mom and Dad are), and all of a sudden, the door opens (of course, Reilly detects it immediately and is barking like crazy—I join in too), and in walks Big Darney with a big bucket in his hands covered by a blanket.

We walk over 'cause we want to smell it, and all of a sudden, the blanket starts screaming. I must've jumped a mile in the air. Reilly leaps back too. What in the world is it?

54

Big Darney sits the bucket down by Mom, and she moves the blanket.

I wanna tell her, "Hey, wait, what's in that screaming blanket?" She better be careful.

The next thing I know, she lifts up this little bitty blanket that is moving and kicking. Me and Reilly step a little closer to see what it is, and she turns it around, and it's a little baby that's so cute.

Mom says, "Reilly and Dexter, this is Zion. He is the newest member of the family, and it is your job to make sure no one ever bothers him."

I move closer and sniff him, and he smells so good. He opens his eyes and looks at me. I am in love. I promise with all I have, I will protect him. Welcome to the family, Zion.

The End

About the Author

Michele Webb is a tenured business professional who is switching gears in life and is now channeling her inner artistic side and has written her first book, *Dexter*! Michele is committed to continuing this series, but she is also expanding her footprint into other literary works.

She is a woman of faith, who believes strongly that it takes a village to raise a child and is excited to see this book help guide children, adolescents, and even young adults adapt into the new, ever-changing dynamics of family life.

Michele resides in Southeast Missouri with her husband, David. Close by is her son, Darnell, and two fabulous grandchildren, Zion and Zamya. And of course, her four-legged friends, Dexter, Reilly, BB, and King.

CPSIA information can be obtained
at www.ICGtesting.com
Printed in the USA
JSHW021040251020
9041JS00001BA/2

9 781662 402470